CHARLES DICKENS

A CHRISTMAS CAROL

CAMPFIRE™

KALYANI NAVYUG MEDIA PVT LTD
New Delhi

Sitting around the Campfire, telling the story, were:

Wordsmith	:	Scott McCullar
Illustrator	:	Naresh Kumar
Illustrations Editor	:	Jayshree Das
Colorist	:	Anil C. K.
Color Consultant	:	R. C. Prakash
Letterer	:	Bhavnath Chaudhary
Editors	:	Divya Dubey Andrew Dodd
Editor (Informative Content)	:	Pushpanjali Borooah

Cover Artists:

Illustrator	:	Naresh Kumar
Colorist	:	R. C. Prakash
Designer	:	Manishi Gupta

Published by Kalyani Navyug Media Pvt Ltd
101 C, Shiv House, Hari Nagar Ashram
New Delhi 110014
India
www.campfire.co.in

ISBN: 978-93-80028-32-3

Printed in India at Rave India

About the Author

Born in Portsmouth, England on February 7, 1812 Charles John Huffam Dickens was one of eight children. His father, John, worked as a government clerk, but was imprisoned during Charles's childhood due to outstanding debts. This forced Charles to support his family by going to work in a boot-blacking factory at the age of twelve.

Although Dickens went on to receive a middle-class education at Wellington House Academy, he continued to work at the factory. These experiences of the different elements of society influenced many of the novels he would write later in life.

In 1827, Dickens left the Academy and began the first in a series of odd jobs, as a law clerk. It wasn't until 1834 that he moved into the publishing world. His first job in this line of work was as a reporter for the *Morning Chronicle*. Two years later, Dickens not only saw the first of his stories published, but also married Catherine Hogarth. By 1837, Dickens's stories had been collected into his first novel, *The Pickwick Papers*.

Dickens first published his novels as weekly or monthly serials, a common practice at the time. It helped fuel his popularity with fans who eagerly anticipated each new installment of his stories. The plight of the poor became one of the major themes in Charles Dickens's novels—a reflection of the bitterness he felt about the way working-class people lived and were treated.

Considered to be one of England's greatest writers, Dickens produced many famous works including *Oliver Twist, A Tale of Two Cities, David Copperfield* and *A Christmas Carol*. Charles Dickens died on June 9, 1870.

GHOST OF
CHRISTMAS PAST
GHOST OF CHRISTMAS
YET TO COME
GHOST OF CHRISTMAS
PRESENT
FRED
BOB CRATCHIT
EBENEZER
SCROOGE
MARLEY'S GHOST
TINY TIM

Marley was dead...
...dead as a doornail. There is absolutely no doubt about that.
This must be understood, or nothing wonderful can come of the story I am going to tell.
GATES HAIL
Ebenezer Scrooge was Marley's sole executor, his sole beneficiary, his sole friend and his sole mourner.
But even Scrooge was not so dreadfully upset by the sad event. Instead, he continued with business as usual on the very day of the funeral...
...on Christmas Eve.

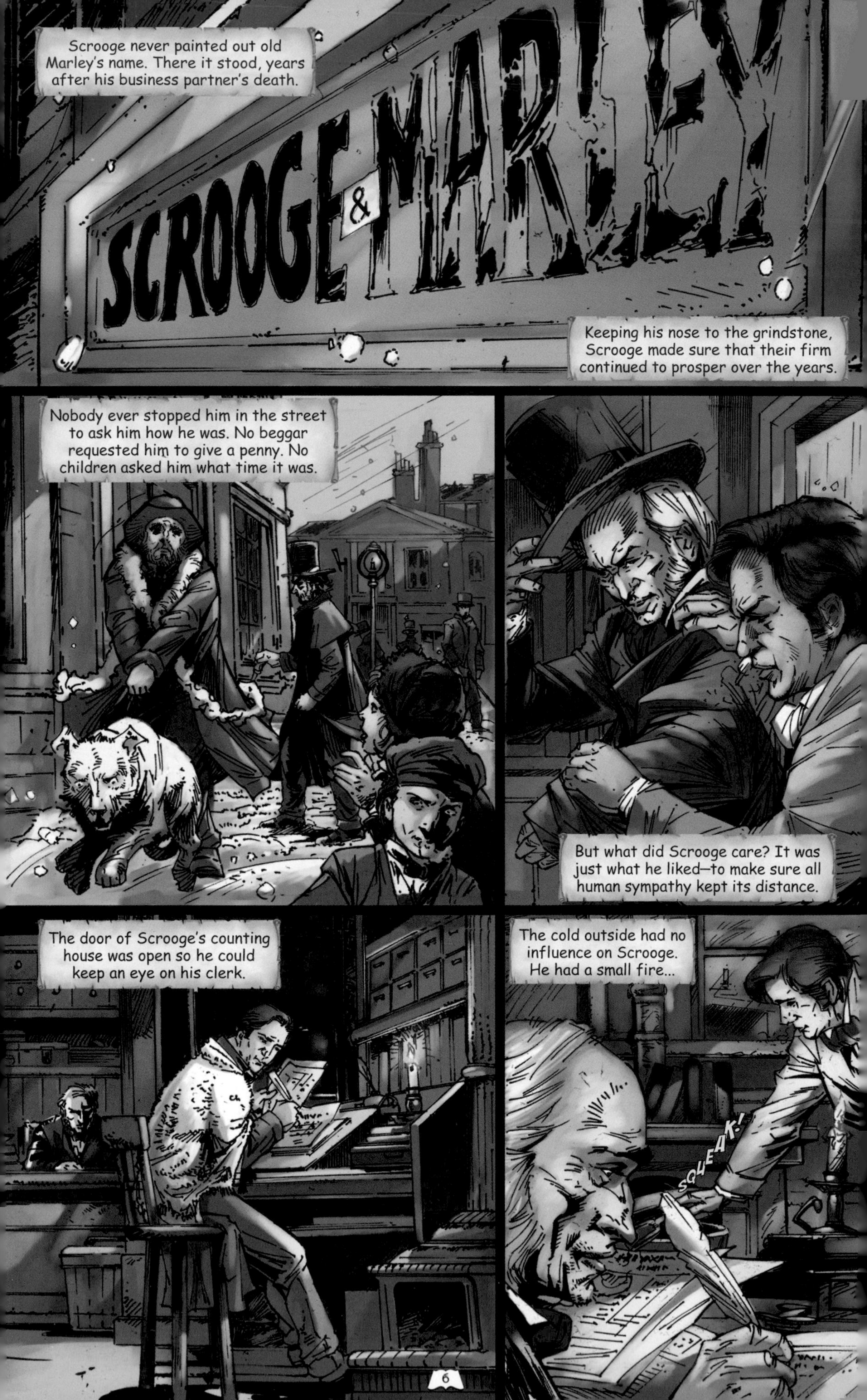
Scrooge never painted out old Marley's name. There it stood, years after his business partner's death.
SCROOGE & MARLEY
Keeping his nose to the grindstone, Scrooge made sure that their firm continued to prosper over the years.
Nobody ever stopped him in the street to ask him how he was. No beggar requested him to give a penny. No children asked him what time it was.
But what did Scrooge care? It was just what he liked—to make sure all human sympathy kept its distance.
The door of Scrooge's counting house was open so he could keep an eye on his clerk.
The cold outside had no influence on Scrooge. He had a small fire...
SQUEAK!

...but the clerk's fire was so much smaller that it looked like one coal. Therefore, he tried to warm himself with a candle.
A Merry Christmas, Uncle! God save you!
Bah! Humbug!
Christmas a humbug, Uncle! You don't mean that, I'm sure?
I do. Merry Christmas! What right do you have to be merry? You're poor enough.
Then what right do you have to be glum? You're rich enough.
Don't be cross, Uncle.
What is Christmas to you but a time for paying bills without money; for finding yourself a year older, but not an hour richer; for balancing your books, and finding every item dead against you?
Every idiot who goes about with 'Merry Christmas' on his lips should be boiled with his own pudding, and buried with a stake of holly through his heart.

Nephew, celebrate Christmas in your own way, and let me celebrate it in mine. It has never done you much good!
Celebrate it! But you **don't** celebrate it, Uncle.
There are many things which might have done me good, but which I have not gained from. Christmas is the only time I know of when men and women can think of others.
And therefore, Uncle, though it has never put a scrap of gold in my pocket, I believe that it **has** done me good and **will** do me good.
So I still say, Merry Christmas, Uncle!
CLAP! CLAP!
CLAP! CLAP!
If I hear another sound from you, you'll celebrate your Christmas by losing your job!
Don't be angry with Mr. Cratchit, Uncle.
You're quite a powerful speaker, sir. I wonder why you don't go into Parliament.
Come! Dine with us tomorrow.
Dine with you? Bah!

But why?
Why did you get married?
Because I fell in love.
Because you fell in love? Bah! Good afternoon!
You never came to see me before I got married, Uncle. Why give it as a reason for not coming now?
Good afternoon.
I want nothing from you; I ask nothing of you. Why can't we be friends?
Good afternoon.
I am sorry to find you so stubborn. I came here with the Christmas spirit. So a Merry Christmas, Uncle!
Good afternoon.
And a Happy New Year!
Good afternoon.

Seasons greetings to you and your family, Mr. Cratchit.
Merry Christmas, sir.
There's another fellow...
...my clerk, earning fifteen shillings a week, with a wife and family, talking about a merry Christmas. Unbelievable!
Scrooge and Marley's, I believe? Do I have the pleasure of addressing Mr. Scrooge or Mr. Marley?
Mr. Marley is dead. He died seven years ago, this very night.
Well, we have no doubt his surviving partner is just as generous.
At this festive time of the year, Mr. Scrooge, we should provide a little for the poor who suffer so much.
Are there no prisons and Union workhouses?
Plenty.

Oh! From what you said, I was afraid that something had happened to stop them carrying out their useful work.
We choose this season to raise funds because it is a time when people desperately feel want.
What shall I put you down for?
Nothing.
You wish to be anonymous?
I wish to be left alone. I don't make merry at Christmas, and I can't afford to make idle people merry. I support the establishments I have mentioned.
Many can't go to those places; and many would rather die.
If they would rather die, they should just do it, and decrease the surplus population.
Good afternoon, gentlemen!
SLAM

God bless you, merry gentleman...
...may nothing you dismay!
Bah! Get away from here!
Run!
And **you** will want all day off tomorrow, I suppose?
If it's convenient, sir.
It's **not** convenient. And yet, you don't think it's unfair when I pay a day's wages for no work?
It's only once a year, sir.

A poor excuse for picking a man's pocket every twenty-fifth of December!
But I suppose you must have the whole day off. Be here earlier than normal the next morning.
Yes, sir. Merry Chrrr-- um... good night, sir.
Scrooge took the melancholy stroll to his dull residence in London town. Nobody lived in the building but him.
Scrooge had not given one thought to Jacob Marley since he had mentioned his dead partner that afternoon.
But then, as Scrooge was about to put his key in the lock, it happened.
Jacob Marley!

BANG!
Bah!
SHHH-LOCK!
Scrooge was not a man to be frightened by echoes.
Darkness is cheap, and Scrooge liked it.
Nobody under the bed; nobody in the closet; nobody in his dressing gown. Quite satisfied, he closed his door and double-locked himself in—something he did not normally do.

Now feeling secure, Scrooge took off his cravat, and put on his dressing gown, slippers and nightcap.
SLURRRP!
His fireplace was an old one, paved with quaint Dutch tiles.
Yet the face of Marley, dead for seven years, appeared on each tile.
Humbug!
As he threw his head back, his glance happened to rest upon a disused bell.
It was with great astonishment and with a strange, inexplicable dread that he saw it begin to swing.
DING
DING
DING

DING!
DING!
DING!
DING!
DING!
DING!
DING!
DING!
DING!
Soon, every bell in the house was ringing loudly. This might have lasted half a minute, but it seemed like an hour.
Then the bells stopped together – the same way they had begun.
They were followed by a clanking noise deep down below, as if someone was dragging a heavy chain in the cellar.
CLANK! CLANK!
BOOM!
The noise grew louder, as though someone was coming up the stairs.
It's still humbug!
CLANK! CLANK! CLANK!
I don't believe it. I **won't** believe it.

CLANK!
CLANK!
CLANK
What do you want with me?

MUCH!
Who are you?
ASK ME WHO I WAS.
Who **were** you then?
IN LIFE I WAS YOUR PARTNER, JACOB MARLEY.
Can y-y-you — can you sit down?
I CAN.
Do it, then.
YOU DON'T BELIEVE IN ME.
I don't.
WHY DO YOU DOUBT YOUR SENSES?
Because a slight disorder of the stomach may affect them. You may be an undigested bit of beef, a crumb of cheese...

There's more of gravy than grave about you, whatever you are!
AAAHHHH!
CLANK!
CLANK!
CLANK!
CLANK!
OOOOOHH...
Mercy! Dreadful apparition, why do you trouble me?
DO YOU BELIEVE IN ME OR NOT?
I do, I must. But why do spirits walk the earth, and why do they come to me?
IT IS REQUIRED THAT EVERY MAN'S SPIRIT MUST WALK AMONG HIS FELLOW MEN. IF THAT SPIRIT DOES NOT DO SO IN LIFE, IT IS CONDEMNED TO DO SO AFTER DEATH.
OH, I AM SO MISERABLE!

I WEAR THE CHAIN I FORGED IN LIFE. I MADE IT LINK BY LINK AND YARD BY YARD; I FASTENED IT OF MY OWN FREE WILL... AND OF MY OWN FREE WILL I WORE IT.
DOES THIS SOUND FAMILIAR TO YOU?
DO YOU KNOW THE WEIGHT AND LENGTH OF THE STRONG CHAIN YOU CARRY YOURSELF? IT WAS AS LONG AS THIS SEVEN CHRISTMAS EVES AGO. YOU HAVE WORKED HARD ON IT SINCE.
Jacob. Old Jacob Marley, tell me more. Speak comfort to me, Jacob!
I HAVE NONE TO GIVE. I CANNOT REST, I CANNOT STAY, I CANNOT LINGER ANYWHERE. MY SPIRIT NEVER WALKED BEYOND OUR MONEY-CHANGING HOLE.
TIRING JOURNEYS LIE AHEAD OF ME. NO REST, NO PEACE. CONSTANT TORTURE OF REMORSE.
But you were always a good man of business, Jacob.

BUSINESS!
MANKIND WAS MY BUSINESS. THE COMMON WELFARE; CHARITY AND MERCY WERE ALL MY BUSINESS!
AT THIS TIME OF THE YEAR I SUFFER MOST. OH, WHY DID I NOT HELP MY FELLOW BEINGS AND SHARE WHAT I CANNOT SHARE NOW?
I AM HERE TONIGHT TO WARN YOU THAT YOU HAVE A CHANCE AND HOPE OF ESCAPING MY FATE.
You were always a good friend to me. Thank you.
YOU WILL BE HAUNTED BY THREE SPIRITS.
WITHOUT THEIR VISITS, YOU CANNOT HOPE TO AVOID THE PATH I WALK. EXPECT THE FIRST TOMORROW, WHEN THE BELL TOLLS ONE.
Couldn't I take them all at once and get it over with, Jacob?
EXPECT THE SECOND ON THE NEXT NIGHT, AT THE SAME HOUR.
THE THIRD UPON THE NEXT NIGHT, WHEN THE LAST STROKE OF TWELVE HAS STOPPED VIBRATING.
DON'T LOOK FOR ME ANYMORE; FOR YOUR OWN SAKE, REMEMBER WHAT HAS HAPPENED TONIGHT.

The apparition beckoned Scrooge to approach the window.
The air was filled with phantoms, wandering here and there in restless haste, moaning as they went. Scrooge had known many of them during their lives.
He had been quite familiar with one old ghost, who cried miserably at being unable to help a poor woman with an infant.
The specter of Marley floated out into the dark night and joined them.
Scrooge closed the window. He started to say 'humbug!' but stopped at the first syllable.

Due to the emotions he had experienced, Scrooge was in great need of rest, so he went straight to bed and fell asleep.
ZZZZZZZZZZ
When Scrooge awoke, it was dark. He suddenly remembered that Marley's Ghost had warned him of a visit when the bell tolled one.
It's exactly one o'clock!
DONG!
Are you the spirit whose coming I was told about?
I AM.
Who and what are you?
I AM THE GHOST OF CHRISTMAS PAST.
Long past?
NO. YOUR PAST.

Please cover yourself with your cap.
WHAT! DO YOU WANT TO PUT OUT THE LIGHT I GIVE? IS IT NOT ENOUGH THAT YOUR PASSIONS HELPED TO MAKE THIS CAP AND FORCED ME TO WEAR IT THROUGHOUT THE YEARS?
I am sorry. I had no intention of offending you.
RISE!
RISE AND WALK WITH ME!
I am a mortal and might fall.
FEEL JUST A TOUCH OF MY HAND TO YOUR HEART AND YOU WILL BE UPLIFTED IN MORE WAYS THAN THIS.

Good heavens!
I was raised in this place. I was a boy here!
YOUR LIP IS TREMBLING. DO YOU REMEMBER THE WAY?
Remember it! I could walk it blindfolded.
IT IS STRANGE THAT YOU HAVE FORGOTTEN IT FOR SO MANY YEARS! LET US GO ON.
As the boys in their country carts trotted toward them, Scrooge recognized every face.
All these boys were in great spirits and shouted to each other, until the area was so full of merry music that the crisp air was alive.
THESE ARE SHADOWS OF THE THINGS THAT HAVE BEEN. THEY CANNOT SEE OR HEAR US.
THE SCHOOL IS NOT QUITE DESERTED. A SOLITARY CHILD, NEGLECTED BY HIS FRIENDS, IS STILL THERE.

Not an echo could be heard in the old school. But, on seeing his younger self, Scrooge began to weep.
WHAT IS THE MATTER?
Nothing. Nothing. There was a boy singing a Christmas carol at my door last night. I would like to have given him something, that's all.
LET US SEE ANOTHER CHRISTMAS.
Scrooge's former self grew larger and the room became a little darker and more dirty. Again, all the other boys had gone home for the jolly holidays.
Dear, dear brother! I have come to bring you home, home, home!
Home, little Fan?
Yes! Home for good. Father is so much kinder than he used to be— home is now like Heaven! We'll be together all Christmas long.

SHE WAS ALWAYS A DELICATE CREATURE, BUT SHE HAD A LARGE HEART.
She did. I cannot deny it.
SHE DIED A WOMAN AND HAD SOME CHILDREN, I BELIEVE.
One child.
TRUE. YOUR NEPHEW.
Yes.
Although they had just that moment left the school behind them, they were now in the streets of a city. It was Christmas time here too.
DO YOU KNOW WHERE WE ARE?
Know it! Of course I know it. I was an apprentice here!

Why, it's old Fezziwig! Bless his heart. It's Fezziwig alive again!
Yo ho, my boys! No more work tonight. Christmas Eve, Dick. Christmas, Ebenezer! Let's have the shutters up before a man can say 'Jack Robinson!'
Dick Wilkins, indeed! He was very much attached to me. Poor Dick! Dear, dear!
There were great festivities that evening as everyone participated in the merriment and dancing. Cake, cold roast, mince pies and plenty of drinks flowed freely into the bellies of all there that night. No money was spared.

Scrooge remembered everything and enjoyed everything. His heart and soul were in the scene.
Scrooge and the spirit overheard the apprentices pouring out their hearts in praise of Fezziwig.
IT'S A SMALL MATTER TO MAKE THESE SILLY PEOPLE SO FULL OF GRATITUDE.
Small?
IS IT NOT? FEZZIWIG SPENT JUST A FEW POUNDS OF YOUR MORTAL MONEY FOR THIS EVENING. IS THAT SO MUCH THAT HE DESERVES THIS PRAISE?
It isn't that, Spirit. He has the power to make us happy or unhappy. The happiness he gives is just as great as if it cost a fortune.
WHAT IS THE MATTER?
Nothing particular. I would like to be able to say a word or two to my clerk just now, that's all.
I DON'T HAVE LONG LEFT. QUICK!
The years change people. I would prefer not to look at this.
YOU MUST.
...it doesn't seem to matter to you. Another idol has taken my place.
Belle, what idol has taken your place?
A golden one.

There is nothing in the world as hard on us as poverty.
You fear the world too much. All your nobler hopes have merged into the one hope of being rich.
One by one your aspirations have fallen. One master-passion now consumes you – money.
Does it not, Ebenezer?
Even if I have grown wiser, I have not changed toward you. Have I?
Our agreement is an old one. It was made when we were both poor and content to be poor...
...until, through patient hard work, we could increase our worldly wealth.
But you have changed. When we met, you were another man.
I was a boy.
There was so much promise when our hearts were one. But, now they are two, it causes so much misery.
I can release you.
Have I ever asked for release?

In words? No. Never.
In what, then?
In a changed nature; in an altered spirit... in everything that made my love of any worth or value to you.
I release you with a full heart, for the love of who you once were. May you be happy in the life you have chosen.
Spirit! Show me no more! Take me home. Why do you delight in torturing me?
THESE ARE SHADOWS OF THE THINGS THAT HAVE BEEN. THEY ARE WHAT THEY ARE. DO NOT BLAME ME.
Take me away from here! I cannot bear it.
Leave me!
Haunt me no longer!

In the struggle, if a situation in which the ghost was undisturbed can be called a struggle, Scrooge noticed that its light was burning high and bright.
He assumed the light was somehow related to the influence the ghost had over him and seized the extinguisher cap.
Scrooge pressed the extinguisher down with all his might.
However, he could not hide the light, which streamed out from under it.
Scrooge became conscious of an overwhelming exhaustion and was overcome by an irresistible drowsiness.
He barely had time to fall into bed before he sank, once again, into a heavy sleep.

ZZZZZZZZZZ
Scrooge awoke and knew, without being told, that it was one o'clock.
He felt restored to consciousness in the nick of time, for the special purpose of holding a meeting with the second messenger.
Scrooge drew the curtains back himself this time, not wishing to be taken by surprise by the spirit.
Now feeling prepared for almost anything, he began to ponder the source of a ghostly light that shone in from the next room.
COME IN!

It was his own room. There was no doubt about that. But it had undergone an amazing transformation.
COME IN! AND GET TO KNOW ME BETTER, MAN!
I AM THE GHOST OF CHRISTMAS PRESENT. LOOK AT ME!
HAVE YOU NEVER SEEN ANYONE LIKE ME BEFORE, OR WALKED WITH MY OLDER BROTHERS?
Never.
Spirit, take me where you want. If you have anything to teach me, let's get this lesson done, so I may benefit from it.
TOUCH MY ROBE!

The ruddy glow of the room at night vanished instantly as Scrooge clutched the spirit's garment. Together, the two now stood in the city streets on Christmas morning.
There was nothing cheerful about the climate of the town, but there was still an air of merriment. Everyone there was having fun and was full of joy.
The customers were all enthusiastic and eager in the hopeful promise of Christmas Day.
The sight of these poor revelers seemed to interest the spirit, and he sprinkled incense on their food from his torch.
Is there a particular flavor in what you sprinkle from your torch?
YES, IT IS MY OWN. I MOSTLY GIVE IT TO THE POOR.

Spirit, where are we going?
WE'RE VISITING THE HOME OF YOUR CLERK, MR. CRATCHIT, WHO YOU PAY JUST FIFTEEN SHILLINGS A WEEK.
What has made your precious father late for dinner? And your brother, Tiny Tim?
And where is Martha? She's half an hour late!
Here's Martha, Mother!
Hurrah! Mother has cooked such a lovely goose, Martha.
Why, bless your heart, my dear. How late you are!
We had such a great deal of work to finish up last night, that we had to clear up this morning, Mother!
Father's coming!
Hide, Martha, hide!

We're home! Merry Christmas, everyone!

Where's our Martha?

Not coming.

Not coming! Not coming on Christmas Day?

Surprise, Father!

Oh, my darling Martha. I'm so glad you're here.

Martha didn't like to see him disappointed, even though it was a joke; so she soon came out from behind the closet door.

I didn't know Bob had a crippled son.
WHY BOTHER TO KNOW?

Bob, how did little Tim behave today?
As good as gold. Somehow he becomes thoughtful sitting by himself so much.
Tiny Tim told me that he hoped the people who saw him in church would remember who made lame beggars walk and blind men see.
I believe he is growing strong and hearty.
Everyone, come to the table.
The goose! The goose! Is it ready, Mother?
Yes. Now, let your father carve it up.
No, you do the honors, Mother.
Mmm... it is wonderful. No other goose has ever been cooked as well as this.
It's the best dinner we've ever had!

It smells lovely, Mother.
Oh, what a wonderful pudding!
This is the greatest success you have achieved since our marriage.
That is a weight off my mind. I was worried about the amount of flour I used.
Everybody had something to say about it, but nobody even thought to mention that it was too small for a large family.
It is sooooo good, Mother.
At last the dinner was done, and all the Cratchit family gathered around the fireplace.
A Merry Christmas to us all, my dears. God bless us.
God bless us all.
Tiny Tim, Bob Cratchit's crippled son, was the last to speak.
God bless us, every one!

Spirit, tell me if Tiny Tim will live.
I SEE A VACANT SEAT IN THE CORNER WHERE TINY TIM SITS, AND A CRUTCH WITHOUT AN OWNER, CAREFULLY PRESERVED.
IF THESE SHADOWS REMAIN UNALTERED BY THE FUTURE, THE CHILD WILL DIE.
No, no!
Oh no, kind Spirit! Say he will live!
IF THESE SHADOWS REMAIN UNALTERED BY THE FUTURE, NO MORE LIKE ME WILL FIND HIM HERE.
BUT, IF HE IS TO DIE, HE SHOULD JUST DO IT, AND DECREASE THE SURPLUS POPULATION.
ISN'T THAT RIGHT?
MAN, IF YOU ARE A MAN IN YOUR HEART, YOU SHOULD NOT SPEAK WICKED WORDS UNTIL YOU HAVE DISCOVERED WHAT 'THE SURPLUS' REALLY IS.
WILL YOU DECIDE WHO SHALL LIVE AND WHO SHALL DIE? IN THE EYES OF HEAVEN, YOU MAY BE WORTH LESS, AND BE LESS FIT TO LIVE, THAN MILLIONS OF OTHERS LIKE THIS POOR MAN'S CHILD.

At the ghost's words, Scrooge hung his head and began trembling.
A toast to Mr. Scrooge, the provider of the feast!
The provider of the feast, indeed! I wish he was here. I'd give him a piece of my mind!
My dear, the children are here! It's Christmas Day.
It must be Christmas Day, if we're drinking to the health of such a hateful, stingy, hard, unfeeling man as Mr. Scrooge.
My dear! It's Christmas Day.
I'll drink to his health for your sake, and not for his. Long life to him! A Merry Christmas and a Happy New Year. He'll be very merry and very happy, I have no doubt!
To Mr. Scrooge.
After drinking a toast to Mr. Scrooge, Tiny Tim began singing in his weak, but pleasant voice.
Silent night...

Holy night...
All is calm...
All is bright...
What places are these?
PLACES WHERE PEOPLE WORK HARD. BUT THEY STILL KNOW ME. LOOK!
Ha ha!
He said that Christmas was a humbug! He believed it too!
That's a shame for him, Fred!
He's a comical old fellow; and not as pleasant as he could be. However, his contempt carries its own punishment.
I have nothing to s against him

I know my uncle is rich, but his wealth is of no use to him. He does no good with it.
I have no patience with him.
Oh, I have. I feel sorry for him. I couldn't be angry with him if I tried. He is the only one who suffers because of his unusual ways.
For some reason he dislikes us and won't eat with us.
Well, he misses out on a very good dinner...
...and some pleasant moments, which would do him no harm.
I pity him, so I intend to give him the same chance every year, whether he likes it or not.
Anyway, it is time for some fun. How about a game of blind man's buff?
Topper, you're 'it'.
Topper has nearly caught that young girl. Go on, Topper.
HA HA!
Topper, stop looking!
Ha ha! He is cheating, ha ha! It has been so long since I've played games.
I wish I could join them.

They are about to start a new game. Give me half an hour more, Spirit.
WE MUST GO. I HAVE OTHER STOPS TO MAKE.
They saw a great deal and went to many places where misery existed.
But each place had a happy ending, as the spirit left his blessing there.
You seem to be growing older by the minute. Are spirits' lives so short?
MY LIFE UPON THIS GLOBE IS VERY BRIEF. IT ENDS TONIGHT.
Tonight!
TONIGHT AT MIDNIGHT. LISTEN TO THE CHIMES! THE TIME IS DRAWING NEAR...
Excuse me, Spirit, but something strange that doesn't belong to you is sticking out from your robe.
Is it a foot or a claw?
IT COULD BE A CLAW, CONSIDERING THE AMOUNT OF FLESH THERE IS ON IT. LOOK HERE!

LOOK DOWN HERE.
NO, THEY ARE MAN'S. THE BOY IS IGNORANCE. THE GIRL IS WANT. BEWARE OF THEM BOTH, BUT MOST OF ALL, BEWARE THE BOY...
Spirit! Are they yours?
...FOR ON HIS FOREHEAD I SEE DOOM WRITTEN, UNLESS IT IS ERASED.
Do they not have any shelter or resources?
ARE THERE NO PRISONS OR WORKHOUSES?
The spirit attacked Scrooge with his own words for the last time.
DING! DING! DING!
Scrooge looked around for the ghost, but could not see it. As the last stroke stopped vibrating, he saw a solemn phantom coming toward him.

Am I in the presence of the Ghost of Christmas Yet to Come?
You are about to show me shadows of the things that have not yet happened, but will happen in the future. Is that so, Spirit?
I fear you more than any ghost I have seen. I know your purpose is to do me good, and I'm prepared to go with you. Will you not speak to me?
Lead on, Spirit, for the night is disappearing fast and I know this time is precious to me. Lead on, Spirit!

Ah! I feel at home, Spirit. We are at the Stock Exchange where profit is worshiped, and I feel alive.
When did he die?
Last night, I believe.
Why, what was the matter with him? I thought he'd never die.
God knows.
What has he done with his money?
I haven't heard. Left it to his company, perhaps. He hasn't left it to me, that's all I know.
It's likely to be a cheap funeral. Do you think we should go?
I don't mind going if a lunch is provided.
Well, I'm not very interested in going as I don't wear black gloves, and I never eat lunch. But I'll offer to go if anybody else will.
Come to think of it, I have a meeting.
Scrooge knew the men, and looked toward the spirit for an explanation.

Leaving the busy scene of the Stock Exchange, the Ghost of Christmas Yet to Come pointed the way into an obscure part of town that reeked of crime, filth and misery.
Spirit, why bring me into a pawn shop in this foul part of town?
Well, well, look at this – a cleaning lady, a laundress and an undertaker.
You couldn't have met in a better place.
Come into the parlor.
What are the odds of seeing you here? Everyone has a right to take care of themselves.
That's true. No one ever looked after themselves more than he did.

Why are we standing around then? Who is worse off for losing a few things like these? Not a dead man, I'm sure.
Indeed not.
If the wicked old screw wanted to keep them after he was dead, why wasn't he decent in his lifetime?
If he had been, he'd have had somebody to look after him when he was struck with death, instead of lying there dying, all alone by himself.
Every word you say is true. It's a poor reflection on him.
Open this bundle, old Joe. Let me know its value. Speak plainly.
I'm not afraid to go first. We all knew that we were helping ourselves before we met here. It's no sin.
No, let me go first. My bundle is very small.

A pencil case, buttons, a broach... hmm... I'll give you sixpence.
Who's next?
Sheets and towels... boots that are in need of repair...
Ah! Little sugar tongs!
One pound, seven shillings and three pence. I always give too much to ladies. It's a weakness of mine.
One pound, seven shillings and three pence! That's all?
If you ask me for another penny, I'll knock off two shillings.
And now, undo my bundle, Joe.

Bed curtains? This means you took them down, rings and all, with him lying there?
Yes, I did. And why not?
You were born to make your fortune.
I don't hold my hand back when I can get something by reaching out.
His blankets? I hope he didn't die of anything infectious?
Don't worry about that. I'm not so fond of him that I'd stick around for such things.
And here is a fine white shirt. I took it off before they buried him in it.
We can make a profit now he's dead because he frightened everyone away when he was alive! Ha ha ha!

Spirit, I see, I see. The case of this unhappy man could be my own. My life is like that now.
Merciful Heaven, what is this?
He recoiled in terror. Beneath a ragged sheet lay something covered up. Though it was silent, it announced itself in awful language.
Then Scrooge realized, it was the body of a man. He lay in the dark, empty house, with no man, woman or child to say he had been kind to them.
Spirit, this is a fearful place.
When we leave here, I shall not forget this lesson. Trust me. Let us go!
I understand you, and I would pull back this sheet to reveal his face if I could.
But I do not have the power, Spirit. I do not have the power.

If there is anyone who feels emotion because of this man's death, show that person to me, Spirit, I beg you.
The phantom revealed a mother and her child who were awaiting news anxiously.
Are we completely ruined?
No. There is hope yet, Caroline.
If he relents there is hope. Nothing is impossible if such a miracle has happened.
He is past relenting. He is dead!
Who will our debt be transferred to?
I don't know. But, before that time, we shall be ready with the money.
We can sleep with light hearts tonight, Caroline!

The only emotion caused by the man's death was one of pleasure.
Spirit, let me see some tenderness connected with a death.
The phantom took Scrooge through the streets that he knew so well, until they reached Bob Cratchit's home again. But this time it was quiet. Very quiet...
...and here is your father at the door!
You went to the cemetery today then, Robert?
Yes, my dear. I wish you could have come. It would have done you good to see what a green place it is.
But you'll see it often enough. I promised him that I would walk there every Sunday.
My little, little child!
Father, don't be upset.

He went upstairs, to the room above.
Poor Bob sat down on a chair beside the child. When he had thought for a while, and composed himself, he kissed the little face.
Tim...
It is okay. We will love you always.
Goodbye, my little child. We'll see you again one day, in Heaven.
He had come to terms with what had happened, and went down again feeling quite happy.

The family gathered together and talked.
You will never guess what happened earlier today. I met Mr. Scrooge's nephew in the street.
He saw that I looked a little down.
He asked what had happened to distress me. I told him about Tiny Tim.
'I am heartily sorry for that, Mr. Cratchit,' he said, 'and heartily sorry for your good wife.'
How he ever knew that, I don't know.
Knew what, my dear?
That you were a good wife, of course.
Mr. Scrooge's nephew gave me his card, and told me that if he could be of any service, to go and see him where he lives.

It really seemed as if he had known Tiny Tim and felt with us.
I'm sure he's a good soul!
You'd be even more sure of that if you saw and spoke to him. I wouldn't be at all surprised if he got Peter a better job.
We will not forget poor Tiny Tim—will we—the first one of us to part?
Never, Father!
And I know, my dears, that when we remember how patient and mild he was, we shall not quarrel easily among ourselves.
No, never, Father!
Specter, something tells me that it is almost time to leave. I know it, but I don't know how.
Tell me who that man was that we saw lying dead.

Spirit, before I go nearer to the stone that you are guiding me toward, answer one question for me.
Are these the shadows of the things that **will** be or are they only the shadows of the things that **may** be?
Men's ways will lead to certain ends if they continue with them...
...but if they change their ways the ends will change too.
Say this is true with what you are showing me!

Scrooge moved toward the stone, trembling as he went; and read upon the neglected grave...
EBENEZER SCROOGE
Am I the man who lay upon the bed?
The finger pointed from the grave to him and back again.
No, Spirit! Oh no, no!
Spirit, hear me! I am not the man I was. I will be a different man as a result of these encounters with you spirits.

Why show me this if I am past all hope?
Good Spirit, please pity me. Assure me that I can still change these shadows you have shown me, if I alter my life.
I will honor Christmas in my heart, and will try to keep it all year. I will live in the past, the present and the future. The spirits of all three will live inside me.
I will not shut out the lessons they teach.
Oh, tell me that I can wipe away the writing on this stone!

NOOOOO!!!
Holding up his hands in a last prayer, he saw the phantom's hood and clothes start to change. It shrunk, collapsed...

...and faded away into a bedpost. And, yes, the bedpost was his own!
This is my own bed! And my own room!
But, best of all, the time ahead of him was his own, to make amends with.
He was so excited, and so full of good intentions, that he could hardly speak.
I will live in the past, the present and the future! The spirits of all three will live inside me.
Oh Jacob Marley! Heaven and Christmas be praised for this!
The curtains are not torn down! They are here, rings and all. They are here!
I am here.
The shadows of things that would have been can be banished. I know it. They will be. I know they will!
I don't know what to do! I am as light as a feather. I am as happy as an angel. I am as merry as a schoolboy. I am giddy all over.
A Merry Christmas to everybody! Hello here! Whoop! Hello!
I don't know what day of the month it is. I don't know how long I've been among the spirits.
I don't know anything. I'm quite a baby. Hello! Whoop! Hello here!
Never mind, I don't care.

A Merry Christmas to everybody! A Happy New Year to alllll the world!
HE HE! HA HO Ho
DING DONG DING DING DONG DONG
Oh, glorious, glorious church bells!
What day is it today, my fine fellow?
Today! Christmas Day, of course!
It's Christmas Day! I haven't missed it. The spirits have done it all in one night. They can do anything they like. Of course they can.
My fine fellow, do you know the poultry shop on the next street?
Of course I do.

An intelligent boy. A remarkable boy! Do you know whether they've sold the prize turkey that was hanging up there?
What! The one as big as me? It's hanging there now.
Is it? Please go and buy it.
You're joking.
No, no, I am serious. Go and buy it, and tell them to bring it here. Come back with the man and I'll give you a shilling.
Come back with him in less than five minutes and I'll give you half a crown!
I'll send it to Bob Cratchit's. He won't know who it is from! The turkey will be twice the size of Tiny Tim.

Here is the turkey.
And here is half a crown. Merry Christmas, my delightful boy.
Thank you, sir. Merry Christmas. You're so kind.
Take this to the home of Bob Cratchit at 25 Camden Town.
But you must take a cab to get there. Here is some more money.
Scrooge walked about the streets, watching people hurrying to and fro, and met them all with a delightful smile.
Then he recognized someone coming toward him.
Mr. Scrooge?
My dear sir, how do you do? You came into my office yesterday seeking a donation for the charities. I hope you were successful.
Yes, that is my name. Although I realize you might not like the sound of it. Allow me to beg your pardon. Would you have the goodness...
And then, Scrooge whispered into the gentleman's ear.
Lord bless me! My dear Mr. Scrooge, are you serious? I don't know what to say...

Scrooge went to church, and walked about the streets, and patted children on the head, and realized that everything could give him pleasure.
In the afternoon, he began to walk toward his nephew's house. He passed the door a dozen times before he had the courage to knock.
Is your master at home, my dear?
He's in the dining room, sir, along with mistress. I'll show you upstairs, if you would like.
Thank you, my love. He knows me. I'll go on in from here, my dear.
Fred! It's me, your Uncle Scrooge. I have come to dinner. Will you let me join you, Fred?
Well, bless my soul!
Merry Christmas, Uncle.
Merry Christmas to you all!
We're so glad you were able to come.
Scrooge received a very warm welcome from everyone, and felt at home in five minutes. It was a wonderful party, with wonderful games, and wonderful happiness.

Scrooge arrived early at the office the next morning. Oh, he was early! He was hoping to be there first and catch Bob Cratchit coming late! And he did; yes, he did!
Hmmm, what time is it?
SQUEAK!
Ahem... Mr. Cratchit? A word, please.
What do you mean by coming here at this time of day?
I am very sorry, sir. I am late.
Yes, you are.
It's only once a year, sir. It shall not be repeated. I was enjoying the celebrations yesterday.
Now, I'll tell you what, my friend. I am not going to stand for this sort of thing any longer.
And therefore...

A Merry Christmas, Bob!
...I am going to raise your salary!
What?
A merrier Christmas, Bob, than I have given you for many a year! I'll raise your salary and try to help your struggling family.
We will discuss your affairs this afternoon over a drink, Bob! Fill up the fires and buy another coal scuttle before you dot another i, Bob Cratchit!
Thank you, sir.
Scrooge was better than his word. He did it all and infinitely more.
And to Tiny Tim, who did not die, he was a second father. He became as good a friend, as good a master, and as good a man as the good old city knew.
God bless us, every one!

ABOUT US

It is nighttime in the forest. The sky is black, studded with countless stars. A campfire is crackling, and the storytelling has begun—stories about love and wisdom, conflict and power, dreams and identity, courage and adventure, survival against all odds, and hope against all hope. In the warm, cheerful radiance of the campfire, the storyteller's audience is captivated, as in a trance. Even the trees and the earth and the animals of the forest seem to have fallen silent, bewitched.

Inspired by this enduring relationship between a campfire and gripping storytelling, we bring you four series of *Campfire Graphic Novels*:

Our *Classic* tales adapt timeless literature from some of the greatest writers ever.

Our *Mythology* series features epics, myths and legends from around the world, tales that transport readers to lands of mystery and magic.

Our *Biography* titles bring to life remarkable and inspiring figures from history.

Our *Original* line showcases brand new characters and stories from some of today's most talented graphic novelists and illustrators.

We hope you will gather around our campfire and discover the fascinating stories and characters inside our books.

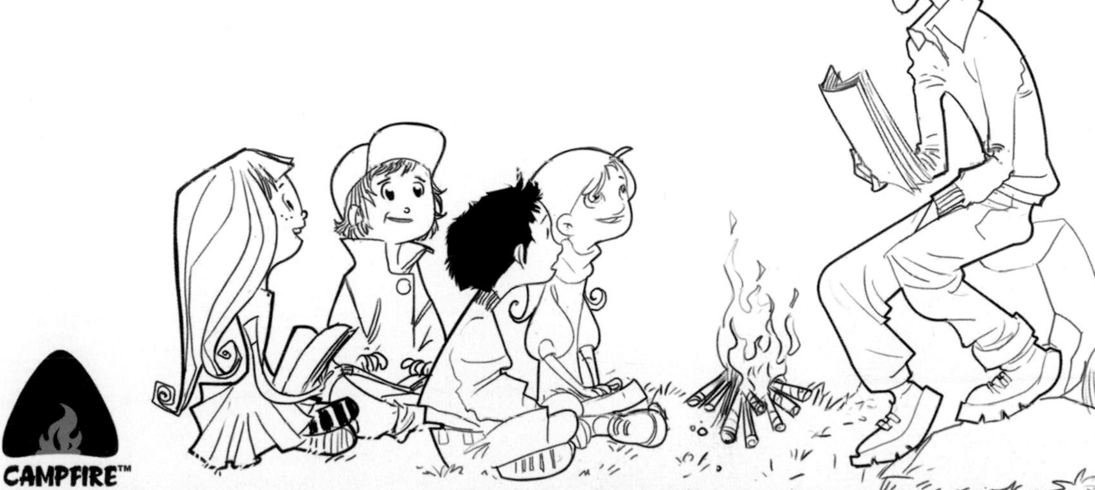

Houses of Horror

A peek at some of the scariest houses in England

BORLEY RECTORY: ENGLAND'S MOST HAUNTED HOUSE

Borley Rectory was built in 1863. As its name suggests, it was the residence of the Borley village rector. It is often said to have been the most haunted house in England because of the spooky events that began taking place there in the early 1900s. People noticed strange smells, the sound of horses, ghostly shadows and areas of the house becoming particularly cold. And a chilling fact is that someone or something actually tried to communicate with one of the occupants in 1930. Marianne Foyster, the wife of the rector at that time, found strange scrawled messages, asking for help, appearing on the walls of the house. Who wrote them? Was it the spirit of a murdered nun apparently buried under the house? Well, no one really knows. Though the rectory was demolished in 1944, its legacy continues, and the site is believed to be one of the scariest places in England.

DID YOU KNOW?

Old tales tell of large black dogs that roam the countryside in England in the dead of night. An omen of death, they are not ordinary dogs, but are supposed to be phantoms with red glowing eyes. One has apparently haunted Newgate Prison for hundreds of years.

THE BROWN LADY OF RAYNHAM HALL

In 1936, two reporters of a magazine went to Raynham Hall in Norfolk, to take photographs of the 17th century house. As they were photographing the staircase, they saw a white, misty figure floating down it. Then they took what is now believed to be the most famous, authentic photo of a ghost. The photograph of the Brown Lady of Raynham Hall! The Brown Lady is thought to be the ghost of Dorothy Walpole. Legend has it that she was imprisoned in the house by her husband in the early 1700s, and it is her restless spirit that haunts it. Those who have bumped into the ghost say it wears a brown dress and has a bony face with dark hollows instead of eyes.

SPOOKY 50, BERKELEY SQUARE

In 1887, two drunken sailors sought shelter for a night in an empty house—number 50, Berkeley Square in London. Do you know what happened next? One of the men was found dead, and the other was found babbling! It is said that they had encountered the infamous ghost which haunted the house in the 19th century. People say the ghost was so frightening, that it literally scared people to death! There was a room on the top floor, called the Haunted Room, from where neighbors reported hearing sounds of furniture being dragged, and ringing bells, even though the house was deserted. Today, the house is occupied by the booksellers Maggs Brothers and is frequented by curious visitors.

THE ROYAL GHOSTS OF WINDSOR CASTLE

Windsor Castle in England is the largest inhabited castle in the world, and is one of the many places where the royal family live today. But do you know that it is supposed to be the home of many royal ghosts as well? While the apparition of Henry VIII has been seen passing through its corridors, the ghost of Elizabeth I, walking around the rooms wearing a black shawl and gown, has also been sighted. George III has also been spotted close to the window of the royal library, where he had been confined when he was alive. Apart from kings and queens, the ghost of Herne the Hunter, a huntsman of Richard II, has been seen many times in the gardens of the castle. Legend has it that he was hanged from an oak tree in the 14th century. His ghost is often seen under, what is considered to be, the very same oak tree!

DID YOU KNOW?

The unnatural and relentless fear of ghosts is called phasmaphobia! The word comes from the Greek words, 'phasma' (apparition) and 'phobos' (fear).